For Lottie and Primrose – L.R.

For Isabella Rose.
Love always Aunty Katdog – K.H.

Lucy Rowland Katy Halford

There's No Such Thing As...
MERMAIDS

SCHOLASTIC

"There's **no such thing** as **mermaids**," my sister said last night.

Today I'll go **exploring**

just to see if she is right.

I've packed my **telescope, my lunch**

. . . there's **such** a lot to do!

And so much **searching** to be done so

could YOU help me too?

There's **no such thing** as **mermaids**.

I've hunted by the stream.

I thought I saw a shiny tail.

It must have been a dream.

There's **no such thing** as **mermaids**.

I looked around the park.

I peered inside the deep blue pond,

but only saw the dark.

There's **no such thing** as **mermaids**.

I tried the pool as well.

I thought I saw one on the slide.

I guess it's hard to tell.

There's **no such thing** as mermaids.

The aquarium was pretty,

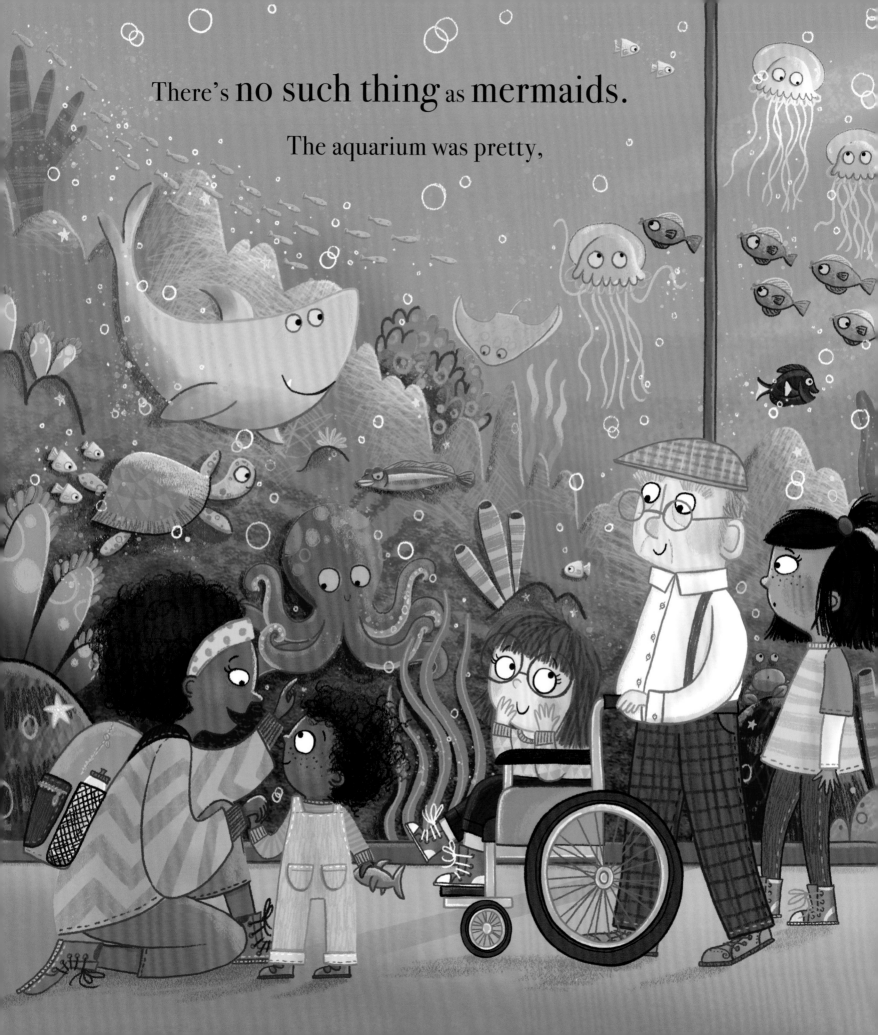

with fish and sharks and turtles

but no mermaids – what a pity!

There's **no such thing** as mermaids.

Next, I looked around the town.

TED'S TOYS

utique

I ate lunch by the fountain
with the water
splashing down.

There's **no such thing** as mermaids.

But I thought I'd try my luck . . .

I rowed out on the lake that day . . .

and only saw a duck.

There's **no such thing** as **mermaids**.

Next, I went to check the sea.

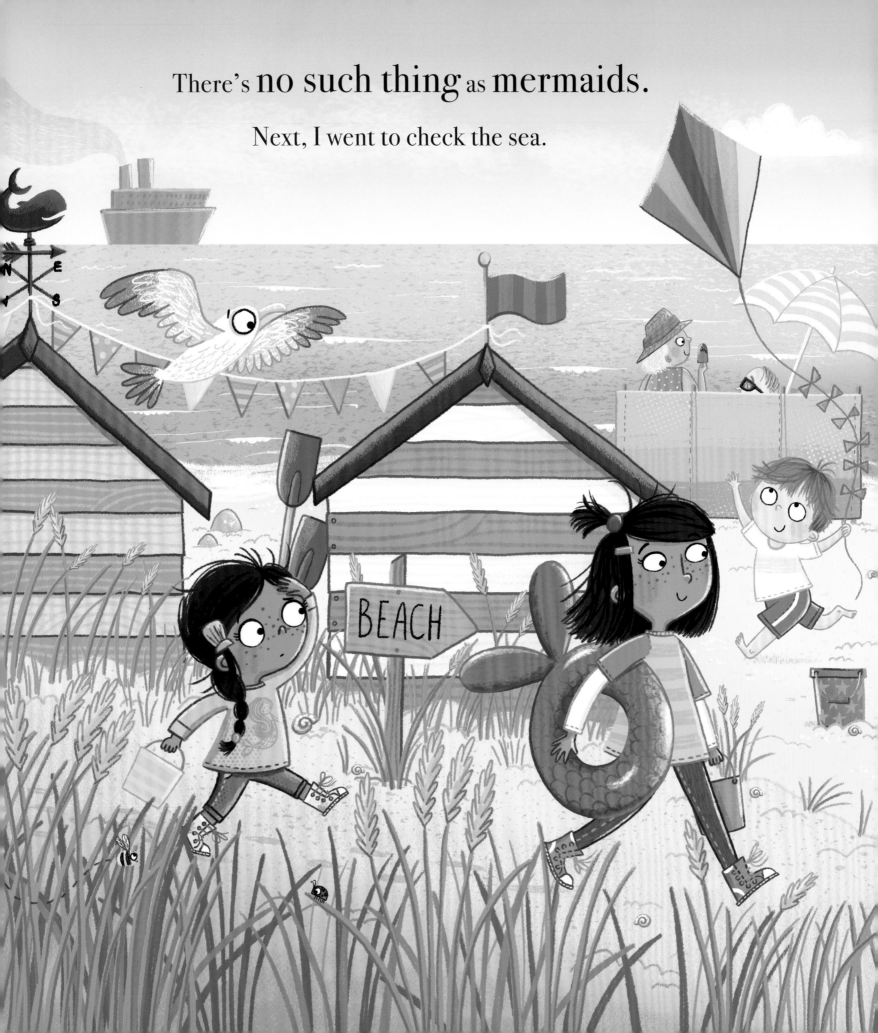

BEACH

I couldn't see one anywhere,

perhaps they're scared of me?

There's **no such thing** as mermaids.

As I rode along the shore,

the rock pools were quite empty

but I'll try just one place more.

There's **no such thing** as mermaids.

In the evening, by the river,

the water grew quite still and cold.

I gave a little shiver.

"Oh there you are!" my sister calls.

"I've looked all round for you!"

"There's **no such thing** as **mermaids**," I explain.

"It must be **TRUE**."

She takes my hand quite gently

and she tells me not to cry.

We watch the fireflies sparkle,

tiny lanterns in the sky.

But as we turn towards the rocks . . .

a glisten in the air . . .

the moon peeps from behind its cloud . . .

A MERMAID!

Over there!

My sister gasps. She blinks her eyes.
She thinks we've got it wrong, but . . .

there ARE such things as mermaids,
and I knew it all along.

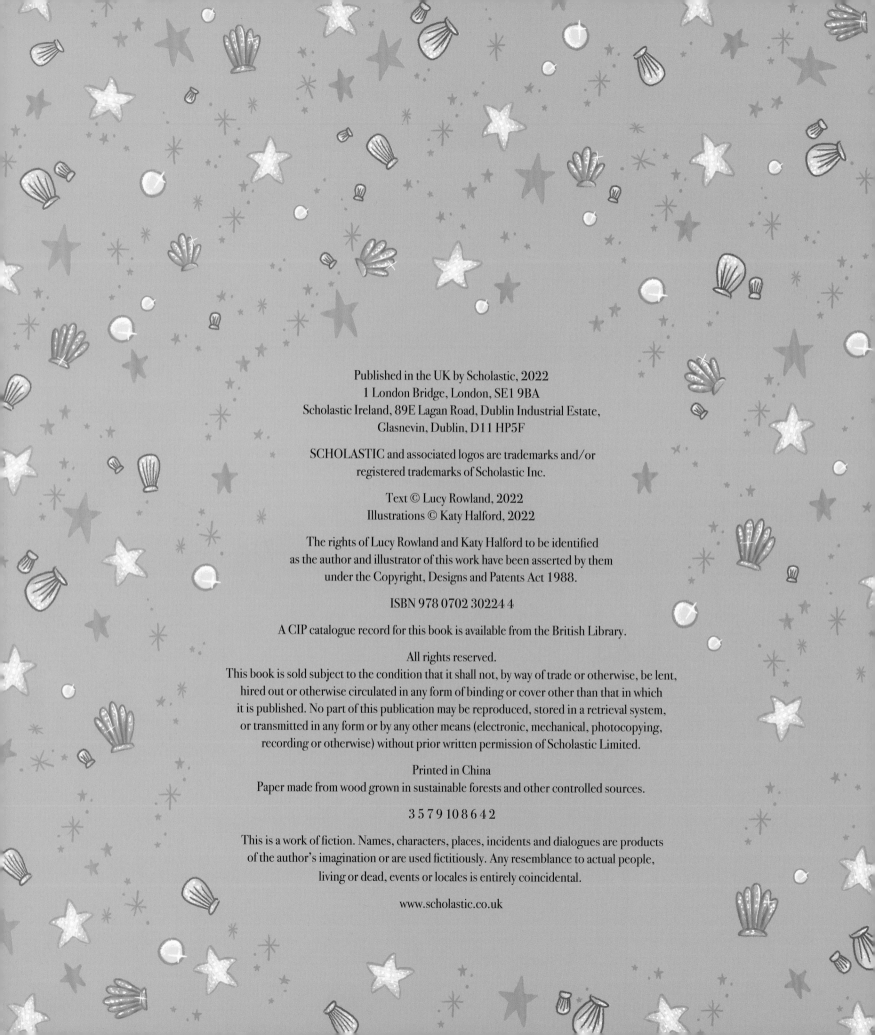

Published in the UK by Scholastic, 2022
1 London Bridge, London, SE1 9BA
Scholastic Ireland, 89E Lagan Road, Dublin Industrial Estate,
Glasnevin, Dublin, D11 HP5F

SCHOLASTIC and associated logos are trademarks and/or
registered trademarks of Scholastic Inc.

Text © Lucy Rowland, 2022
Illustrations © Katy Halford, 2022

The rights of Lucy Rowland and Katy Halford to be identified
as the author and illustrator of this work have been asserted by them
under the Copyright, Designs and Patents Act 1988.

ISBN 978 0702 30224 4

A CIP catalogue record for this book is available from the British Library.

Printed in China
Paper made from wood grown in sustainable forests and other controlled sources.

3 5 7 9 10 8 6 4 2

www.scholastic.co.uk